Copyright Notice:

Read it!
Integrate it!
Live it!
Truth, that is...

Feeling the fullness, owning one's entire experience; an internal disposition of consent with oneself, that is the foundation. Forcing other's rests on the basis of forcing oneself. Living in a depth of willingness to acknowledge the interior reality constructed, the gateway to freedom.

Cōnsēnsiō

In latin, cōnsēnsiō is the nominative singular form of the word that translates to "consent". In practice, it can mean agreement, accordance, assent, harmony, unanimity, plot, conspiracy, among other things. Herein this allegorical anecdote, it is left to the reader to parse the intended inferences.

For those who desire gentleness, compassion, and safety in all things intimate…

…you are not alone!

Chapter 1

Her fingers stroked the skin of his chest. His heart quickened its pace. Her head lay resting on his shoulder as their legs entwined. "What is your desire," he asked her.

"This," she whispered, continuing to gently caress his skin. Blood began to enlarge the soft erection he had been laying with as they cuddled.

Feeling a pulse in her chest as his energy began to shift, she moved her hand to his stomach, centimeter by centimeter. Breathing in all the sensations as she moved.

Deep, full breaths flowed through their lungs. Inhaling the aromatic energies of each other as flowers in bloom. With each breath, his wand of light became larger, and stood taller. Her temple of feminine magic became ever-more moist. His wand pulsed. Her temple throbbed.

Flames of desire burned in them. Deeper. Hotter. And with greater intensity as each breath fanned the erotic energies coursing through their bodies.

Shifting his head to look into her eyes, "I desire you," he said extending the full magnitude of his spirit. Her body softened in his arms as she allowed the energy of his words to wash through her.

She looked at his lips. He looked at hers. With great slowness, their lips met with the softness of two clouds merging into one. Electricity flashed through their bodies as lightning flashing through clouds. The electricity energized their skin as it arced through them, raising hair as it went.

Her vulva pulsed as sacred fluid began dripping from her. His shaft quaked as the pre-essence of his sacred fluid slowly emerged out of the tip. Their tongues began to explore each other's as the energies ripened into a furnace of merging desires.

She shifted her leg across his body. He reached across her back to her hips and pulled her to lay on top of him. Her legs wrapped his hips as his tip met her vulva. The flames of desire roared in their groins. Hers softened to receive. His flexed to penetrate.

They looked into each other's eyes and both inhaled a full breath. Not moving, they allowed the moment to be. Placing no expectations on the other, they each met the fullness of their desire with breath.

Breathing in the sensation of her outer vulva caressing his shaft. Without entering, they lay looking into each other's eyes.

Breathing.

His hips began undulating as her hips began rotating. The baritone of his moaning reverberated through her chest, causing her shoulders to soften. She melted onto his chest. Her hips stopped rotating. The desire to have him enter was all that she could bear.

"What do you desire," he asked.

"I want you in me," she said. Smiling a sensuous grin. He gently kissed her forehead. "My body aches to have you," she continued.

"Breathe it all in," he said as his hands slowly pressed into her buttocks. "Allow yourself to feel the depth of desire in you, as it is."

"How do you hold this desire in you without following through," she asked.

"Breathe. Deeply," he said. "Shift the focus of your mind's vision from seeing me enter you, to visualizing the electricity in your hips rise into your heart. Feel for the slightest sensation of the energy rising from your hips into your heart." He paused all of his movement and hugged her closer to him. "Feel my breath and match it as best you can."

Her body rose and fell with the force of his breath expanding and collapsing his chest cavity. Placing the tip of his middle finger on the base of her spine, he stroked up her spine as they inhaled in unison. "Feel this sensation and guide your vision. Raise each energy pulse in the temple of your femininity, to the temple of your heart." Her body shivered as his finger stroked her spine.

Reaching the middle of her back, just over her heart, he brought all fingertips together with softness on her skin. Spreading his fingers apart across her back, over her heart, his hand flattened. His palm, and all of his fingers gently resting on her back. Each of their chests continuing to rise and fall as they breathed in synchronicity.

With slight movement, her shoulder blades spread further apart. Reaching greater relaxation, she released a soft moan. "I want you," she whispered. Her legs began spreading to receive the pinnacle of his desire.

He placed his hands on her hips, pausing the motion, "If we do this, we are opening to another layer of intimacy." He paused. "Have you spoken with your husband about this?" The corner of her eyes turned down as she quickly looked away from his eye. A constriction flushed through his chest, tightening his stomach.

"I told him I need more space to explore," she said, the heat dissipating from her chest, turning to a knot in her stomach.

"And is he okay with that," he asked as he felt her grip on his chest release.

"Not exactly, but he says he understands that I need to do what I need to do. And if this is part of that, he'll try to be okay with it. I don't know if he'll ever truly understand. But I don't feel what I used to feel for him, and he says he knows he's changed since we were young and doesn't want to keep me from what I need to grow." Slowly leaning back away from him, "Why is it so important to you that he knows?"

Pausing, a small smile turned the corners of his mouth as he gazed into her eyes. "Clarity in the space we are creating here. My desire is to connect with you in the deepest way possible. I want to feel all of you. To know the totality of you. And I can't bring myself to fullness without a fullness in honesty. My emotions are held only for those who can bring an equal degree of honesty to this space."

She looked away in brief contemplation, "Integrity, right?"

"Yes. I'm not willing to accept anything less. In simple terms I will not take part in dishonesty to any degree. That this is difficult for him is one thing. Him not knowing is something else entirely. He may not want to know every detail, which is fine. But him having the understanding that you have no restriction on your exploration is what You desire, is the most important thing. I want to support you exploring your desire." Smiling, he raised his hands with the softness of clouds resting atop a mountain, cupping her jawline in his hands. Gazing into her eyes, "I desire you in your fullness. You opening to this honesty with him, is you opening to a fullness of emotional integrity in yourself. My desire for you is a desire to connect with you in all ways; physically, intellectually, emotionally, spiritually."

He paused, allowing his words to permeate in the space between them. She looked into his eyes, and smiled saying, "I don't know what it is about you, but I don't know that I would have been able to talk to him about this without your wisdom. You make me think about things I've never thought before."

Smiling, he said, "I'm attracted to a free mind, and a vulnerability in emotions, more than I am to a sexy body. I can find a sexy body on any street in the world. But a free mind, that tends to bring with it an emotional depth that is worth more than all the gold in the world." He smirked, "And it just so happens that it's an exceptionally pleasurable combination of factors in a woman. So, you could call me selfish. I desire your intellectual freedom. Your emotional vulnerability. Your physical presence. And the rawness of you in your sexual power. The combination of those things is a multidimensional universe of pleasure not possible without honesty in every one of those dimensions."

"Stop, you're making me cum," she said lightly slapping his chest as she giggled.

With delicate movement, he reached in and cupped her face in his hands once more. "May I kiss you," he whispered. Smiling, she closed her eyes and moved her lips to meet his in soft embrace. His tongue gently touched her upper lip as he slowly pulled back. Sucking her lower lip, he softly bit down pulling her lip with him as he went.

A surge of energy flushed through her body. Her hips began moving. His wand pulsed to attention meeting her moist vulva.

He moved one hand to the back of her neck as his other arm wrapped around her back. Her arms wrapped around his back. Her nails pressed into his back, "I want you to take me."

Chapter 2

He looked out at the 12 people in front of him. Formed in a half circle 12 feet from his position, they each sat with a folder in their laps. The front of the folders was emblazoned with large bold print, center justified down the full front of the folder, *Do Not Open until requested to do so*. Behind him on a marker board were the words, *Only in silence can we have dialogue.*

All eyes were on him. A deafening silence filled the room. One of the 12 bounced her knee in anticipation. Another strummed the folder in his lap with his fingers. He sat, waiting for a volunteer to step forward.

One minute passed with no one speaking.

Two minutes passed.

Three minutes in a gentleman of maybe 40 years, with wisps of gray hair creeping up the side of his head, finally broke the silence, "Are we waiting for something to begin?"

"We are waiting for you," came the delicate voice from an assistant facilitator in the back of the room. All eyes turned toward her voice, only to be met with a gentle face, smiling in response.

Taking the cue, the facilitator sitting up front said, "Please open the cover of your folder to the first page and the only first page." As they opened it, they were met with another page inscribed with large bold letters down the front, *Participants Only. Proceed only in response to a request to do so.*

"It is apparent that you desire to be here," the head facilitator said. "If not, why would you be sitting in these seats." He paused for a moment of reflection on the rhetorical question. "Unless you are under some form of duress, or have been coerced in some manner, you being here constitutes the result of decision made by you. That said, if any of you are under duress, or have been coerced to be here, please see myself or an assistant facilitator at the break and we will help you find legal counsel for your situation.

"At any time, at the behest of your own volition," he continued, "and without notice, you have the freedom to opt-out of continued participation in the events that go on here this weekend. That said, forward from this point, please understand that your continued presence here implies in fact that you are an active participant in creating the eventual result of what happens here this weekend.

"Now, that said, who here would like to restate what you've just heard," he asked. The eyes of the participants quickly darted around at one another. Some frantically working back and forth in expectation of someone else offering to speak first. Several moments passed, and a hand rose. "Please, if you will," the facilitator said, "Stand and restate for us what you have heard."

A woman, short in height, with shoulder length auburn hair and hazel eyes began to speak, "It seems to me that, what you're saying is, if we want to stay here, we have to participate. Is that right?"

He let the words fill the air, pausing several seconds before giving reply. "It is not for me to tell you if it is right," he said. "I leave that to all of you. You are the ones who've paid nearly a thousand dollars to be here. Is there anyone else who wishes to add to what was heard?" Another hand rose, "Please stand, and state for us what you've heard."

A man, about 6 foot tall, athletic in build, brown hair tightly trimmed around his ears faded up to the top of his head, stood up. "I'm not sure I heard what," he leaned forward slightly to see the name tag of the woman who just spoke. "I'm not sure I heard what Eileen heard, though I'm not discounting what she heard. My understanding of what you said is that we are under no obligation to be here if we don't want to be here. My question is, if that's true, and we decide to leave, does that mean we get our money back?"

Again, the facilitator paused to let the words fill the air. "That seems a practical question. However, before I respond to it directly, I would like to allow more space for others to offer what they've heard. Is there anyone else here who would like to speak to what was said regarding your freedom to opt-out?"

Several more people offered a reflection of what they heard. Each met with a pause after the statement. Until finally, several minutes of silence had passed with no one offering anything more. "I will assume by the silence here that those of you who have not spoken have heard a reflection that accounts for what you've heard in my statements. Is this a fair assumption for me to hold at present, or would any of you like to add anything further?"

Silence was all that was heard. "I will take it to mean, then, that the silence indicates that we have come to a common understanding of what your continued presence here means, based on the statements of recount by those who spoke.

"Now to the question of reimbursement. The non-refundable deposit will not be returned. That secures the time of the assistant facilitators behind you. In addition, for every meal, and every night spent on premises here, an additional expense will be prorated for the logistical considerations needed to use the facilities here. If you would like to see a schedule of expenses as a line item description of cost to conduct this retreat, you can request that from any one of our facilitators. Transparency in all dealings here is absolute.

"That said," he continued, "Only if you stay here to the end do I, as facilitator, receive any net profit from you. Meaning, only if you receive value here, do I receive any monetary compensation for my efforts here." He paused, allowing a moment for the last statement to fully register. "Another way of saying that is, for me, the value in me being here is to facilitate your movement toward a fuller experience of your sensuality. I don't benefit unless you do. There is no win-lose here. The structure of this retreat is built on the premise of win-win or no deal."

Several heads tilted in contemplation of the statement. "Why do you suspect that is important to what we're discussing here today?

The idea of win-win or no deal." A few moments of silence passed before a hand rose. "Please, rise," he said, gesturing for the participant to stand, "and let us hear you."

"Well, it seems to me, based on what I saw in the advertisements and sales process to be here, as well as the statements on the folders, and pages, and whiteboards, and the way you're taking it very slowly here, that you're making it a point to both get us to come out of our shell, and come to an agreement. But more than that, it seems we have to like, you know, I'm not sure how to describe what I'm feeling, but it seems like you want us to own this process. And that you're not going to tell us what the right way to do it is, or the wrong way to do it." She paused for a moment, then continued, "So I'm not even going to ask you if what I just said was right, because it'll probably lead down another 10 minutes of you asking others what they heard." Smiling at him with a sly smile, she sat back down.

"Perceptive," he said. Several other hands shot up in the air. Looking at each of those whose hands were in the air, he said "So, I believe we've come to a crossroads here. It seems to me that there is a movement of activity here such that we can begin. That said, if you're all willing, please take the participants only page that your folders are open to and pass it to the left." As he said that, an assistant facilitator walked to the person at the left end of the half circle and collected the papers.

"With that common consensus, please understand that you have given your explicit assent to continue here as an active participant in the events of this weekend. Again, to restate, at any time, at the behest of your own volition, and without notice, you have the freedom to opt-out of continued participation in the events that go on here this weekend.

"Now, with that order of business closed, if you will, please stand and join me in some movement of our bodies as we begin to explore the embodiment of sensuality."

Chapter 3

Profile after profile passed to the right under his thumb. The desire in his belly had been building the past few hours. *What do I want to do with this*, he thought to himself. *You could breathe with it*, he thought as he saw himself in a lotus pose breathing fire up his spine. *Or you could go work out, or you could pleasure yourself.* All options he'd pondered numerous times at this point.

What I really desire is to connect with a woman who has passion. The desire in his belly surged. Countless profiles had passed under his thumb at this point. Some left. But most of them to the right. His criteria were based on what he felt when seeing a smile. Little else mattered to him as the initial context for interest. The resonance of joy in his body as he saw the woman's smile was the guide.

Even if it was only a deep dialogue with a woman of passion, he thought. *You could always text someone you already have context with*, he rebutted to himself. *True, but I enjoy the unknown.* The inner dilemma he was creating for himself served only to deepen the tensions in his body.

Inhaling a full breath, his exhale released into a deep sigh. Tossing his phone to the side, and standing up from his bed, he looked out the hotel window to the darkness above the city lights. *Go for a walk, and connect with people out there, away from your device.* Moments later his shoes were on and he was walking out the door.

The silent buzzes in his pocket indicated activity from one of his apps, *I'm not going to open it till I talk to at least one person on the street for more than 1 minute.* The tensions in his body subsided only slightly as he walked. Breathing deep as he walked, he pulled the energy into his heart with his mind's eye. Feeling a warmth radiate in his chest, the tensions in his groin felt as warm water running through his hips. *Walking always helps.*

Another buzz in his pocket piqued his curiosity. *So maybe just walk for a bit, get some fresh air, then check your phone.* The raw desire in his stomach was impossible to ignore. Inhaling a deep, full breath, raising his shoulders as high as he could, lifting his rib cage off his lungs, the pressure in his groin released a subtle pleasure into his hips.

Where's the closest coffee shop, he thought. *I could go for some chai tea. And maybe I'll meet someone there.* Reaching for his phone, *don't open any dating app, just the map.* Seeing 4 notifications from two different dating apps, his chest tightened with anticipation. His jaw flexed, exerting his will to avoid opening the app. *Go get tea. Flirt with the barista, and maybe another customer. Then check the app.*

Or, you could check it now and potentially begin a conversation there while you walk. Contemplating his options while searching for a tea shop, the closest one was a few blocks away. His pace quickened as his stride lengthened. Focusing into his hip flexors, he inched every bit of extension from the joints he could. Two soft buzzes vibrated in his pocket indicating a text message. Opening his phone to the text app, he saw a message from an old friend. "Hey, just a random drop-in. I hope you know how much you mean to me. You've helped me face things in my current relationship I was too afraid to even verbalize to anyone. Hope all is well in your world. Just wanted to share my gratitude."

He tapped back, "You're quite welcome. There is only one way to experience freedom in relationship, and that is through honesty. And no matter how hard the conversations may be, honesty always leads to the light of clarity, which is what everybody needs. As for my world at the moment, just strolling through downtown Portland, looking for someone who enjoys flirting... you know me ;)"

"Lol, yeah... you definitely are a flirt... lol."

"I mean, when you're as smart as I am, it's hard not to have great jokes."

"You mean when you are a smart ass like you are ;P"

"Hey, sarcasm is an indicator of high intelligence. It's a scientific fact. :D"

"It's a scientific fact that you're too smart for your own good. Knowing you, I bet you're probably strolling through downtown because your swipe right life is leading nowhere."

"Hahaha… I still don't know why we never got together. I couldn't hide anything from you even if I tried."

"I'm way out of your league. You know this. I'm too much a Barbie Doll for you. You and your thing for hippy women. You can't say I didn't want more. I let you know I wanted more, but as you said, I'm too civilized for you."

"Hahaha, touché."

"I hope you find your connection."

"All I need is a deep dialogue with a random stranger, and I'm good."

"I'll never understand your obsession with randomness. Maybe it's just a phase. I really do hope you find what you need."

"Thanks. Truly! Hope you have a good rest of your evening."

"Love you."

"Love you more."

"Stop it."

"You first."

"Whatever… enjoy your evening."

The several minutes of texting found him waiting in line at the tea shop. Pulling his head up from the phone for the first time, he scanned the room. Seeing a cute barista with her hair tied up by her dreadlocks, he began looking at her style so he could complement of her fashion. He found a point noticing her fingernails painted the same color as her earrings, as well as subtle shades of the same color in her shirt. Heat flared up into his chest as a soft pleasure rippled into his shoulders. Inhaling deeply, he took a step closer as the customers in front of him continued submitting their orders. *Don't psych yourself out dude, just relax.* With one customer left, he caught the eye of the barista and half smiled. She quickly looked away, smiling. She wrote the previous customer's order on the cup and handed it to the next barista to finish. He stepped forward slowly as she came back to the register.

"Good evening, how may I help you," she asked placing her hands on the register.

Softly laughing to himself at the thought that just randomly popped into his head, he smiled and said, "I'm not sure, do you have any special drinks you'd recommend. Kinda in the mood for something new. Do you have a favorite drink?"

"Uhm, well, they're all good. I don't have one I don't like. Do you have a favorite flavor or anything?"

"I usually go with chai tea, but that's just my go to when all else fails. I guess I'm kinda curious if you have any drinks that you like to make. I mean, it seems to me that you're an artist so I'm kinda wanting to experience an artist at work." The customers behind him began to shuffle with impatience. Smiling to himself, *I'm not choosing till I leave my compliment.*

"I don't know that I'm an artist, but I do like the *Chai Tea Authenticity*," she said. "Instead of using a chai concentrate, we make it from scratch with a little of this and a little of that. It takes longer, and costs a bit more, but it has more love brewed into it so it's totally worth it."

Laughing he said, "Sold. Can't say no to a little more love in my life. As for you being an artist, only an artist will match the color of her fingernails, to her earrings, to the secondary color in her shirt. That's type of style is artistic fashion. And the dreadlocks is just icing on the cake."

Smiling, with a hint of red in her cheeks, she input the order as she said, "Thanks. I guess I never thought of it that way."

"Yeah, well, that's kinda the thing with artists. They have a tendency to just do what they do and not think too much about it. Anyway, thanks for the recommendation."

"You're welcome."

He moved to the end of the counter to wait for his drink.

Another barista behind the counter locked eyes with him for a few seconds. She half smiled and looked down to the cup in front of her. "Ah, the authentic chai. One of my favorites."

"Yeah," he said intoning a question. "Will you be the one filling it with love?"

"You know it. It's the only way to do it right."

"Nice. That's what I like to hear." Noticing a necklace with shells, made of braided and knotted rope, he pointed to it on her neck and asked, "Is it like a prerequisite to be a hippy to work here."

Slightly laughing, she said, "Yeah, well it definitely doesn't hurt. I'd say it's a requirement to be eclectic. We have a lot of different breeds here, emo, punk rockers, hippies, and even some barbie dolls. But we're all interesting people. It's the only way I know to put love into things. You gotta have substance."

"Right on," he said. "I can get down with that. So how long have you worked here?"

"Since we opened, so about 5 years," she said as she turned to the back counter, grabbing several different spices from the back shelf.

"So you must enjoy what you do here. And it looks like the most elaborate chai tea process I've seen yet. How many spices is that?"

Looking up with a piercing glare into his eyes, "Well, that's a trade secret. I could tell you, but then I'd have to hire you."

"Wait, hire me. Does that mean you run this joint?"

"Well yeah, that's my name on the sign, of course I own it," she said with a wink. The chatter of the customers and orders in-process around them faded to the background. It was just him and her caught in conversation.

"Okay. Okay, I see you. Working it like a boss," he said. "But, as much as you probably want to hire me, I'm not sure you could afford me," he said with a cheesy grin.

"Oh god. Not one of those. Too cocky for his own good."

Laughing, he said, "Nah, I just know my worth. If I did work here, there'd be too much boss behind that counter between the both of us, and it likely wouldn't work out, or I'd just eventually buy you out."

"Oh you think so huh. That sounds like a challenge."

"Only if you like a good challenge."

They both looked at each other and laughed. Smiling, she said, "You could be fun."

"Yeah, it's not a could be. It's a guaranteed thing."

"You sure are high on yourself. How do you fit your head through those doorways."

"Easy. I respect boundaries. It's the best way to keep an ego in check. It also helps that I make it a point to explore the depths of others. I like to experience others in their fullness. That tends to guarantee others enjoy their time with me."

"You sound like a hippy."

"Probably because I am one. Even though I'm not dressed like it presently, I can go business professional to hippy in 3 seconds flat."

Laughing, she said, "I never heard that. You might have to show me sometime."

"Well, maybe if after I finish my tea and decide if there was enough love in it, I'll leave you my number and we can continue this conversation later."

"There's no question on if there's enough love in it. I made it. And you must have me mixed up with someone else, I don't date random people that come into my shop."

"Well that's good, because it wouldn't be a date. More like an experience," he said laughing with a cheesy grin.

"You're definitely extra right now. You know that right."

"I'm always extra. I have more love to give than I know what to do with. That's why you should hire me, but can't afford me. You wouldn't know what to do with all the extra love you'd have on tap."

"Oh trust me," she said rolling her eyes, "I have all the love drama I need up in here. And here's your drink."

"Thank you. That's quite a long process to make chai tea."

"Yeah, well, that's why it costs as much as it does. And it doesn't help that I have a rude customer talking my ear off the whole time," she said winking with a smile.

"Oh, rude huh? That's how you like to play?"

"It is," she said with a sly grin. Before he could retort back she was already heading over to the register barking out to get the next order. She looked back at him, shrugged her shoulders slightly, and smiled as if to say, *the ball is your court bud.*

Shaking his head, softly laughing, he grabbed his drink and he went to the patio and looked for an open table near the doorway with the most traffic. He'd long since changed his tendency to hide himself in the furthest table removed from humans, and decided that to enjoy human connection, its best to put yourself close to humans.

It wasn't till the phone in his pocket buzzed that he remembered the notifications. The events of the last several minutes had distracted him from the tensions that lead him to the coffee shop. Opening the phone to a dating app, he saw three new likes. *Well alrighty then.* Opening to the first profile, he saw nothing in the about me, and only one picture. He clicked to the message and wrote his standard message to those profiles without words and little to go on, "Hey there, how's your day going so far?" He knew it was a bland message, but without substance to the profile, he always started with small talk as the first step.

Moving to the second profile, he flipped through all the pictures. Each one was a close up selfie of the same head shot nine different times. *Ok then, this one clearly likes variety.* Reading her profile she indicated that she wasn't interested in hookups, emphasizing it by writing it in all caps. Further down, she identified herself as Ravenclaw. *Finally, substance.* Clicking to the messages, he typed in, "So if you're Ravenclaw, and I'm Slytherin, does that mean you hate me, or would you be willing to overlook my lust for power?" *She probably won't respond to that.* He said to himself. Retorting to himself, he thought, *Yeah, maybe. But if she does, it'll allow me to cut through the small talk.*

As he began to tap into the third profile, he was interrupted by another barista. One he'd not interacted with yet. The barista pulled a rag from his apron and moved to wipe the table down. As he wiped, he asked, "Enjoying your tea?"

"Yea, I am actually. It's definitely in the top three chai teas I've ever had. It could use a little more love though," he said with a smirk.

Laughing, the barista said, "Don't let her hear you say that. That's one of her specialties. She puts a lot of stock in that drink. She's actually won some awards with it."

"Well, you can tell her that it's in my top three. Not the top, but definitely top three."

"I'm not gonna tell her that. I like my job," he said half joking, half serious.

"She seems like she can be a ball buster if she needs to be. How is she as a boss?"

"Yeah, she's definitely not someone to cross. But at the same time, she'll go out of her way to make sure you're taken care of if you're her employee. If you're dedicated to being the best barista you can be, she'll have your back. And she pays better than any other coffee shop around. That's why everyone wants to work here. But if you slack, or half-ass it, she has no problem letting you know. I've seen some people quit on day 2 because of it. But most of us have worked here for years"

"Interesting. Good to know. Does she have a boyfriend or husband?"

"Uhm, that's a definite no," the barista said, chuckling.

"What do you mean by that?"

"You talked to her. The men who try have no idea how to

take her bluntness. I have no issue saying she's definitely too much woman for me. Maybe someday I could date a woman like her, but I'm not sure I'd want to. If you get between her and her businesses, that's the quickest way to get the ax."

"Wait. Businesses. She has more than one."

"Yeah, this is just her hobby business. She's also a real estate investor. She owns like three or four apartment complexes around town. And she also has several different fast food franchises. She comes here to work when she wants to relax. This is her day off."

"Well how about that," he said in his southern accent. " I appreciate the information."

"Yeah, well," the barista stuttered, "If you're bold enough to try, and you get anywhere near kicking boots off, you're gonna have to let me know how it is."

"Nah, I don't do that. That'd be between me and her. But how about this. Give me your pen." The barista handed him a pen. He took a napkin and wrote, "The tea was okay. I've had better. If you want chai tea excellence, give me a call, and I'll show you how to really put love into it." Writing his number at the bottom, he handed the note and the pen back to the barista, "Give her this for me."

The barista read the note. "Hell no, I'm not giving her that. I told you I like my job," he said laughing.

"I'll make you a deal. If you give it to her, I'll give you a spot, at no charge, in my next workshop on embodying sensuality."

"Embodying what," the barista asked, confused.

"Here, go to this website," he wrote out a URL on another napkin. "Check it out on break. Then give her that napkin."

"I don't know man," the barista hesitated.

"Answer me this. Do you enjoy dating, flirting, and relating to those you consider your love interests? Or is it an awkward experience you try to get through as fast as you can, and into a more stable relational posture?"

"Uh, yeah, I don't flirt, and I hate dating."

"Yeah, so, give her that note. She won't fire you. Then come to my next workshop."

"How do you know she won't fire me?"

"Because she won't. Just trust me."

"I don't know man."

"Look, if she does, you have my number. Call me, and I'll give you a year's worth of wages. I can't make it any easier for you."

"Why don't you give it to her yourself?"

"Because that's not what she wants."

"How do you know that?"

"Come to my workshop and I can go into detail. But in short, especially women like her, they want you to be direct without being direct. If I give her the note, I'll be trying too hard. If you give her the note, I'm using her people to do my job for me. And what I'm trying to communicate is that doing it myself is beneath me. She may take that several different ways, and not see it the way I'm intending it. It's a risk in there being a miscommunication. But I'm curious how she will receive it. And I want her to know that I'm interested in her, but also not overly interested. It's clear she has zero room in her life for a needy men. So, I'm giving her both indifference and interest. It may work, it may not."

"I think I understand," the barista said. "You definitely have bigger balls than most."

"No, I'm just not attached to the outcome. There's a lot of freedom in that my guy. That freedom can be intriguing to women from an emotional perspective."

"Yeah, I'm not sure I know what that means, but I'll take your word for it."

"Hey, look, do yourself a favor. Give her that note, then come to my workshop."

"Ok, but how will you know I gave it to her."

"Because she's gonna contact me."

"I don't know man. I guess we'll see."

"We will bro. We will." Standing up, he looked inside to catch the eye of the hippy with dreadlocks. She happened to look up and see him. He raised his cup and mouthed, "Thanks". He turned to the barista at his table, "Hey, tell that girl with the dreads I said thanks for the recommendation, it was pretty good. And if your boss happens to be in ear shot, all the better."

"You're one schemin dude, you know that right?"

"Yep, it's the only way I know how to be. Hey, you have good rest of your day bud. Good talking to ya."

"Ya, you too man."

Chapter 4

Two days had passed since he left his number with the barista. Spaciousness filled his chest as he stood looking over the vista of the city from his perch atop the hotel's rooftop bar. The indifference he felt this evening as compared to two nights previous was not a new juxtaposition for him. The satisfaction achieved in having a conversation with her was in itself an accomplishment in his book. Rewind his life by 15 years, and the crippling anxiety he experienced when even thinking of approaching a girl was a far cry from where he now experienced himself.

Clarity in desire was the greatest gift he had ever given himself. Having spent over 20 years being consumed by an addiction to pornography never allowed him to know his own desire. Having been snared by the perpetual winds of the latest fad in porn kept his mind and body active in ways he was ignorant to its true impact.

His contemplation was interrupted as the breeze across the rooftop carried an aroma of lavender with it. Shifting to his right, he leaned against the plexi glass rail that surrounded the rooftop as he looked to his left to identify the source of the fragrance. Unable to, he pulled his legs down from the stool they were perched on, and shifted to left more fully to see the entire expanse of the rooftop.

The scent of lavender captivated him. This was not a manufactured fragrance. This was the true aroma. The real essence of the flower. Taking time to visit the luscious lavender fields of northern Oregon was always on his to do list when he visited Portland. The fragrance was both his weakness and his strength. His go-to essential oil in any aromatherapy session. The fragrance in the air now, however, had an overpowering sweetness to it. His chest both melted and ignited in flames as he inhaled the aroma. *Who is wearing that*, he thought to himself.

Out of his periphery, a woman wearing a lavender designed, flowing, shoulderless dress appeared from behind a gentleman in a slate blue windowpane suit. His eyes widened as he realized it was her. The centerpiece of his desire from two days previous. *Well call me uncle Frank and slap me silly*, he laughed to himself. *Game time.*

Making a trip the bar to refresh his cabernet, he appeared to be completely unaware of her while walking in a line to the bar she was sure to see him. He finished with the bartender, and casually turned. With a small step, he moved to the edge veranda covering the bar. The slowness of his drink of dark red liquid extended the indifference he was privy to only moments earlier. As if she didn't exist, he took a step back down the two small steps onto the expanse of the rooftop. Retracing his steps back to his seat, a few feet from the group where she stood, he looked up into the group.

Her eyes were already locked with his. An almost invisible smile on her face. As his eyes met hers, he let out an audible laugh loud enough for most the rooftop to hear, and definitely loud enough to interrupt the man in the windowpane suit who was speaking to what appeared to be his business associate.

All eyes were on him now. "Well how about that," he said to her. "What kind of good graces am I in with the gods to enjoy this kind of synchronicity?" Sidling up to the group of three, "So what brings you to this fancy joint," he said to her. "You more than just a regular old hippy, that's for sure." Reaching his hand to the man in the windowpane suit, he interjected and exchanged names with the two in business suits.

"Well, if you must know," she said, "I'm working a deal on a piece of land to expand my lavender farm."

His head suddenly tilted in recognition that it was her that was wearing the fragrance. So taken by the fact of seeing her here, he forgot about his pursuit of finding the source of the aroma. "Of course its you wearing that audacious amount of lavender isn't it. It smells alright by the way. I was somewhat taken by it a moment ago. Is it your own product?"

"I'm sorry," the high class suit man said, "how do you two

know each other?"

"Oh, he was a churlish customer who came to my coffee shop a few days ago and tried telling me how to make my chai tea."

The two men started laughing, clearly understanding the significance of that particular drink to her. The other man said, "So you think you have a more marketable product in that niche?"

"No, it's not a matter of thinking I do. I know I do," he said. "But that's not what's important. What's important is that she thinks I might," he said winking with a sly smile. "And you two gentlemen seem to know as well as I do that she can't back down from a challenge to her uniqueness."

Both men laughed as if they knew all too well the truth of the statement. "It would be a challenge," she said, "If it was more than words. It seems all he's skilled at is throwing words around. What is it that you do again?"

He raised his glass, holding it by the stem, and slightly tipped it in her direction, acknowledging the acumen of her ability to read a person. "I'm an artist, of sorts."

"What does that mean, 'of sorts'," the man in the windowpane suit asked.

"Well, take this situation for example. In a single laugh, I've completely changed the trajectory of the conversation you all were previously having. So in a sense, I create new types of interactions between people. I guess you could say I facilitate collaboration."

"Again," she said, "throwing words."

Ignoring her, he looked to the other man, and back to the man in the windowpane suit, "So you two have possession of some land she wants. Is that correct?"

"It is."

"And have you all come to terms?"

"Not yet," one of the men said.

"And the condition that's keeping the transaction from executing is," he said, extending the last word as if to allow any one of them to speak.

"I'm not sure that's your business," she said.

"You're right, it's not," he said to the three. "But as you've indicated, my ability to 'throw words' could be what's needed here. I call it 'reframing context', but that's beside the point. In any case, I may be able to see things from a perspective such that you three can execute this deal."

"And you'd do that out of the kindness of your own heart," one of the men asked.

"Sure, why not. I've got nothing better to do," he said, shrugging his shoulders. "So to be clear, I hold none of you to any fiduciary responsibility, and require no fee for my negotiative services rendered here this evening, so long as, if you're not able to come to a mutually reciprocal agreement with my help, you continue on without me after I leave."

The two men looked at each other, and the man in the windowpane suit said, "Seems like you know how to navigate this type of conversation." He turned to her, "What do you think?"

She looked at his smug smile as he held his wine glass. "My mind tells me to have you piss off. But my intuition is telling me to give you a shot. And my intuition hasn't led me wrong yet. You've got 30 minutes."

He raised his glass to her again and winked with his sly smile. "So, the condition that you have yet to align on. Who wants to go first and fill me on what it is? As well as the nature of the contention as you see it."

For the next 20 minutes, the group of four haggled back-and-forth, coming to final terms. Through the course of the discussion, it became clear she carried heavy emotional investment in her farm operations. It had been years since he'd seen someone as passionate as she was about her purpose in life. The warmth in his chest as he heard her speak into her vision was almost intoxicating. Bearing his resolve to remain neutral to the negotiation empowered his fortitude to a degree he had not felt in many years.

He could feel the conversation coming to a close in favor of all parties. He glanced at her, and to most, her composure was steel. To him, however, the extended gaze of her eyes as she took in a deeper than normal breath, tilting her head to him ever so microscopically as she turned her eyes to the man in the windowpane suit communicated volumes. He knew she was on the edge of her seat. She lived for this.

Desire ignited into a raging fire in his body. Taken by the intensity, he forced his mind back to hearing the words of the discussion. "It seems we have a deal then," one of the men said. All three looked to the unexpected fourth of the evening as he passively sipped his wine, slowly nodding his head in agreement.

"Looks like that's what," he looked to his watch, "22 minutes. That's gotta be a new record for me," he said. The sinister smile on his face was made of pure conceit.

Her audible laugh at his overwhelming arrogance surprised even her. She simultaneously could not stand it, and could not resist it. He intrigued her in ways few men could. That he knew what he was doing made it all the more intense. She knew he knew exactly what he was doing. His indifference. His arrogance. His actual ability to negotiate. Pulling every one of her strings for which she was powerless to control the response in her body. The combination of his disinterest in her, and his confidence in what he was doing made it impossible for her to resist him.

"I'll have my assistant send over the contract tomorrow," the man in the suit said.

"Yeah, of course," she said in a hastened tone. "I'm sorry, if you gentlemen will excuse me. I need to use the lady's room." She excused herself from the group. The three men continued chatting. A few minutes later she returned.

The aroma of lavender floated through the air with a renewed vengeance. His nostrils took over as his inhale slowed to a caterpillar pace. Deep into his lungs the fragrance intoxicated his entire being. The two men ceased to exist. The rest of the bar fell from his consciousness. It was only these two agents of embodied passion.

"Well gentlemen," she looked at the two in suits, "I don't want to hold you if you have other business to attend to. And I don't want to cut this evening short, but I have some additional items I need to attend to." She quickly looked at the intruder of her well planned evening. He stood seemingly aloof to her statement. "If you don't mind, I will excuse myself now."

The throbbing in his body intensified as she turned to leave, wanting her to not go. He turned back to the two in suits, "I believe I'll call it an evening myself gentlemen. It was a pleasure doing business."

"Likewise," one said. "Here's my business card. Give me a call next time you're in town. I believe there are some other negotiations you would be well suited to facilitate if you're available. And it wouldn't be pro bono next time."

"Thank you. I am most certainly open to continued business here in this lovely city." He raised his glass to the two, "Gentlemen," then, took a small step backwards, and turned to leave. Placing his glass at the bar as he left, he felt two small vibrations in his pocket indicating a text. Pulling his phone from his pocket, he saw a text from an unknown number from the Portland area code. "What hotel are you in," it read. Laughing to himself, he typed back, "This one of course. Meet me at the bar in the restaurant on the lobby floor."

He proceeded to the lobby floor, making his way to the bar. His heart beat faster as he saw her sitting at the bar. A fresh bottle of wine in hand. Approaching her, he said, "That's a lot of wine for one person."

She glared at him, saying, "You know full well this isn't for one person."

He smiled at her, "Shall we continue the conversation here, or would you like to come up to my room."

She looked at him, raising her left eyebrow at him as if it say, *really*, and said, "You have to ask." He smiled and extended his elbow to her as if to escort her as an usher to his room. She linked her arm in his and they made their way toward the lobby elevators.

Chapter 5

"So, where'd you get my number," he asked. "Do I have to worry you might be a stalker."

She slapped his arm, "You'd hush your face if you knew what was good for you."

"Oh really," he said. "Sounds like you want to get physical," his laugh that followed his statement was an unexpected reaction.

She rolled her eyes and shook heard, "Only if you're lucky."

"I mean, you're the one in my room after texting me, soooo, yeah. About being lucky, I call it being skilled."

"You are such a conceited ass; you know that right."

He only smiled. Taking off his shoes he began to gently place them at the entrance to the room, "So, are you going to continue to track in the dirt of the world into the sacred space of my bedroom, or, you know, perhaps remove your heels?"

"I don't know that I'm comfortable yet. For all I know, that could be a ploy for you to get me to start taking off my clothes."

"I don't need to try to do that. You already want to do that."

"Ha, yea, right. You wish. I could just as easily leave."

"Well, yeah. There's the door. That's always an option here." He finished placing his shoes. "I see two glasses in your hand, and one bottle of wine. Would you care to pour, or would you like me to as you take off your shoes?"

Handing the bottle and glasses to him, he began to pour a translucent red pinot noir. "Pinot, that's always a safe bet. And local too. Nice."

She kicked her shoes half-hazardly next to the precise placement of his. "So, what is it that you do, really," she asked.

Laughing slightly, handing her a glass of wine, he said, "I actually am an artist. I have yet to meet an art form that I don't like. I grew up painting and drawing. Then I found writing, and just kinda meandered through all sorts of things. And I honestly haven't found one that I can't do. It's actually been one of the bigger struggles of my life. Figuring out which one I was most passionate about, to devote my attention to it. Along the way I found out that I enjoy business, entrepreneurship, coaching others, and guiding conversations through the business landscape. So I do a little of this, and a little of that. A somewhat convoluted answer I know. But that's just kinda the nature of how I've come to be here."

"So, you're a professional hippy. Is that what you're saying," she asked. They both laughed.

"Yeah, I guess you could say that." He sat down on the couch, "Care to sit. I promise I don't bite, hard," he said winking. She rolled her eyes as she stepped toward the couch. "So what about you. How have you come to own all these businesses?"

"My dad," she said. Pausing, she looked out the window and said. "He worked as an international real estate executive and built up his own portfolio of properties as well," her voice intoned a slight tremor as she spoke. A wave of emotion washed through his body as he sat listening. She looked back at him, and continued, "When I was eighteen, as a birthday gift to me was a 6-unit apartment in the town my mom and I stayed in, and five thousand dollars in penny stocks. He told me I could sell it all, take the money, and do with it what I wanted. Or take a year before going to school, move down with him, and he would teach me everything he could in that one year about managing real estate and trading stocks and options."

Tears had begun filling her eyes, the tremor in voice had dissipated though, and she was as calm as ever. "My mom and him split when I was young, and he was constantly traveling so I never really got to see him much. I jumped at the chance to spend time with him. I didn't really care about the money. I just wanted to spend time with him." She looked at her listener with a puzzled expression, "I don't know why I'm telling you all this. I've told literally no one this story. I think it might be because you remind me of him. He was a complete ass like you are. The cockiest son of a bitch I've ever known."

His face lifted into a gentle smile, "I'm honored to receive your vulnerability. I sense there is a great deal of emotion here with you and your dad."

"Yeah," she said with a pause. "He died a year-and-half after I moved down with him." She paused again. Looking away from his gaze, she inhaled deeply. She reached up and wiped her eyes. Taking one more deep breath, she turned back to meet his eyes. "In any case, I learned everything I know about real estate from him in that year and a half. I still own that 6-unit apartment. At this point I don't think there's any chance of me disposing of it. I use it to rent to single mothers who have left abusive relationships. Most of them aren't even able to pay rent. I guess it's my way of helping others get a leg up in the world the way my dad helped me." She paused, smiled, and continued saying, "I try to mentor them as much as I can. I've seen some of the women go on to do amazing things. One became a lawyer and is now working in the District Attorney's office specializing in prosecuting cases involving domestic abuse."

Tears filled her eyes once more. He reached for her hand resting on her knee. He cupped her fingers in his, and said, "You clearly care deeply for those you look after. The barista I spoke to at your coffee shop said as much. But I see now what he means."

"I'm usually not this emotional," she said. "I've learned to keep them for myself. As much as women have been able to carve out a lot progress, it's still largely a man's world in my line of work. I look forward to the day I regularly negotiate with women."

"Well," he said emphasizing a southern drawl in his voice, "It's like they say, emotions are the magic of life. Without 'em, that ain't no experience at all."

She looked at him puzzled, "Yeah, uhm, that's not something people say. That sounds like some hippy-ism you just came up with and generalized it like its common sense."

He smiled a guilty smile. Avoiding a response, he took an

extended sip of his wine. She continued, "So what about you? What brings you here? And don't give me that vague 'I'm an artist' crap."

"Well, you know," he said, "I like Portland. So I thought I'd just come hang out for a week. And I guess 'see the sights', as they put it."

"Bullshit," she said. "Now you're purposely feeding me a vague line just cuz I told you not to. Why are you really here?"

Laughing, he said, "You got a good bullshit detector, I tell ya that right now. There were a few times you pushed back in that negotiation calling them on what felt like a bluff. It was entertaining to watch." He raised his glass as if in acknowledgement of her skill and took another long sip.

"So tell me, why are you avoiding the question," she asked, clearly perturbed.

He took a deep breath. Setting his glass on the coffee table, he turned his body more toward hers. "This is always a bit awkward when I first tell someone, and I haven't yet figured out how to say it, so, I'm just gonna say it." He took another breath, "I'm a gigolo."

She looked at him with curious eyes, as if she almost believed him. She slapped his shoulder, "You're full of shit is what you are." He burst out laughing.

"Yeah, I only aspire to be one," he said smiling. "In all honesty, I do actually do a lot of different things. And answering this question always feels like winding through a rabbit hole that doesn't ever really answer the question. But, to be succinct, I'm in Portland because I held a workshop on embodying sensuality to a group of 12 people."

Her eyes squinted. She was searching for any recognition of disintegrity in his statement, but found none. "Hmm," she said. "What is 'embodied sensuality'," she asked emphasizing the phrase.

"Well, take you for example. It's clear you have a passion for doing what you just did up there tonight. Embodied sensuality is about being aware of the sensations in your body at a primal, root level. Rather than mentalizing an experience where you describe it in metaphors with 'like' or 'as'. Embodying your sensuality is about becoming aware of the sensations as the sensations present, hot, warm, rigid, soft, expansive, etcetera. So, like up there tonight, when you looked at me with an extended gaze toward the end, I just allowed the sensations to be as they were rather than trying to figure out what they meant. What I felt was an immense joy for being exactly right where we were, doing exactly what we were doing. And I know that feeling wasn't mine. It was yours."

Taken aback by the acuteness of his description of the feeling, her body leaned away from his slightly. "So you're empathic too then," she asked. His mouth turned up in a smile indicating a humility. Followed by his eyebrow raising indicating his sense of confidence. He tipped his head slightly nodding in agreement. "Alright then Mr. Confident, what am I feeling right now," she said challenging him.

"Well that's easy. You're feeling that you want to strip me naked and taste every square inch of my body."

"Ha!" The volume of her laugh surprised even her. A rush of heat flushed through legs, hips, and up into her chest as the visual he stated ran through her mind.

"See. My point exactly," he said winking. He took both of her hands in his and stood up gently pulling on her hands as he did. Pausing a moment, her face washed over with a submissive smile. She uncrossed her legs and stood to meet him, face to face. Their eyes met. The energy between their lips was magnetic.

One corner of his mouth raised in a half smile. He slowly lowered his head to hers. She responded in kind, bringing her lips to his.

Time ceased to exist. Both his heart and hers exploded in a surge of energy flushing through the whole room. He felt the edge of his body blend with hers. She felt her body be engulfed by and immense space.

He reached for her hips. Lifting her in the air, she wrapped her legs around his waist. Their lips remained sealed to each other's. Their tongues continued writhing in pleasure.

He stepped to the bed. Bending over, he laid her down. Their mouths broke the seal. She scooted back to the top of the bed, stripping her dress off as she went.

Unbuttoning his pants, he dropped them to the floor. He lifted his shirt over his head and threw it aimlessly into the room. Leaving his underwear on, *I'll give her the pleasure of removing those* he thought. Kneeling onto the bed, he moved up to meet her legs. Lifting her foot, he brought his lips to the top of it with a soft kiss. His tongue softly caressed the space between her foot and the beginning of her shin. She giggled with delight, "You're dangerous."

"Maybe", he said, "It might also be that I enjoy desiring you." She scooted her head down from the headboard, lying flat on the bed. The knee of her other leg fell open, revealing the fullness of her feminine temple. He slowly ran his hands up the entire length of her legs. Reaching the top of her hips, his fingers curled around the edge of her panties. Slowly pulling as he kissed her inner thigh, she raised her hips allowing the fabric to easily slide from under her. Raising her legs up, he continued to pull as she did. He gently raised them to his face, slowly inhaling the fragrance as he would a flower. His exhale opened into a baritone moan. She saw his erection increase as he did.

"That's kinda hot," she said. "So you're not one of those guys that's afraid of a woman's odor?"

"Ha! God no. Are you kidding me. Pheromones are real. And enjoy them immensely," he said winking. He took another inhale of the panties then tossed them over his shoulder. "But, there's no comparison for the source of that magic." He reached to her knee picking it up. Placing his tongue on the inner knee, he slowly made his way down her leg using his tongue to taste her as he went. Reaching the top of her inner thigh, at the outer perimeter of her temple, he moved over to her other leg at the same height. He moved down that leg to her knee, tasting her has he went. Her hands roaming herself as he worked. "You taste delicious by the way," he said.

"When are you gonna fuck me," she asked.

"All in due time," he said smiling. "There's a whole buffet of delicacies yet to enjoy." He moved her leg toward her other and laid down next to her on the bed. "Like I said, embodied sensuality is what I do."

"So you like foreplay?"

"I could play all night. There's a wealth of pleasure that can be revealed when you take orgasm off the table."

She turned her head to meet him eye to eye, "What are talking about, take orgasm off the table. What kind of shit is that?"

He smiled. Paused. And slowly moved his hand to her face. The delicate touch he held her with melted her shoulders. He looked at her lips. She looked at his. A moment later their tongues were once again writhing in pleasure. He moved his hand to her back, holding her. Several minutes passed as they explored each other in this way.

Reaching down to her lower back, he wrapped his hand under hip and lifted. Rolling, he pulled her on top of him. Their lips and tongue continued enjoying each other. His chest washed over with pleasure as her nipples pressed into his. Opening her legs, wrapping them around his hips, she pulled back slightly. Moving the exploration of her lips to his chin, to his neck, to his ear. She took the opportunity to begin tasting him.

To his chest. To his nipple. To his ribs. To his stomach. Grabbing his underwear, she pulled them down and off. She moved down to his hips continuing her exploration. To his legs. And back up to his lips and tongue. Laying back on top of him, she reached down and pulled his masculinity up to her femininity. He reached to her hips, held them in place, and asked, "Where are you at in your cycle?"

"What do you mean? I should be having my period in a week

or so if that's what you're asking."

"Yeah, just wondering where you're at in your fertility cycle. I enjoy kids, but I'm not trying to have any right now."

"Do you have a condom?"

"I do. But I'm also desiring to go slower with you. I very much enjoy kissing you. And as fun as it would be to have sex, I desire to get to know your vagina more intimately."

"What does that mean," she asked.

"I want to taste you. To feel your sensitivity with my fingers. To explore your temple with touch so I can know you more fully."

"You're not normal. You know that right."

He smiled a mischievous grin, and asked, "What do you desire?"

"I want you to dominate me. Fuck me. Slap my ass, hard. And take me like a man."

"Well," he said, "It seems we may be at an impasse. I don't really desire those things. However, if you're saying you desire me to be in my primal power, that I can do. But for me, that's doesn't include violent sex."

She could feel his erection waning. Confused, she asked, "I don't know what you mean. Most guys are already finished at this point. And the rest will just continue fucking me."

"Well, I hate to break it to you, but I'm a little bit on the weird side. That whole dominant submissive game, or even just getting straight to sex, fucking, ejaculating, and being done, it's not something I do." He reached his arms around her back in a partial hug. "The best way I can describe it is, inasmuch as you want me to be a man and fuck you, I want you to be in your wild, rawness, and ravage me. But that doesn't mean I want you to just have your way with me and do whatever you want regardless of how it impacts me. I want to meet your wilderness with my power. I don't want to fuck you and just have you take it. I want to elevate your freedom to have you own your raw, wild self on levels you have yet to discover. And I want to do that by being in the fullness of my power, filling you completely."

As he talked, she felt his erection coming back to life. "I don't know that I've ever experienced what you're talking about. But I want to."

He smiled. Bringing his hands to her face, he held her with a gentle touch. "I want to give you that. But to do so, we have to go slower. A lot slower. I need to feel you. And to do that, I need to touch you with great sensitivity. Before I can fill you completely, I need to have a deep sense of the space that I'll be filling." He paused allowing her a moment to take in what he was saying, then said, "Are you okay with that?"

Several moments passed as she looked at him, pondering his statement. Feeling into herself. "I don't know. I'm feeling all kinds of emotions right now. Emotions I don't allow myself to feel with men. This is all new to me."

"That's okay. If you need to take time to feel through this, there is no rush. That's what I mean by taking orgasm off the table. There's no destination to get to other than being here. Now. Completely."

Tears began to fill her eyes, "What the fuck is wrong with me. I'm crying now. I'm sorry. I don't know what's going on."

A soft smile turned the corners of his mouth. "Emotional vulnerability is a powerful thing. It something our rational mind can't comprehend. And it's something that we simply get to witness. And, there's nothing wrong with you. You have nothing to apologize for. If I'm being selfish, you feeling this depth is what I desire."

"Okay. But I don't know. I'm having feelings for you. Feelings I haven't had for a long time. Not since my highschool boyfriend I lost my virginity to."

The reflection of her statement hung in the air. Silence filled the room. "May I ask how that relationship ended?"

"What? Why," She asked perplexed.

"I'm not trying to pry into private information. I'm curious if it ended badly, and if it has left a mark on you."

Her head leaned back slightly, intrigued that he cut right to it. "Well, he wanted me to stay. We were in love. And had been planning on going to the same college together. But I needed to go be with my dad." A tear rolled down her cheek. "He was angry. He wasn't there to see me off when I left. And I haven't seen him since. But I needed to know my dad. And looking back, I can't say I would do it differently."

"That's a big deal. There's a lot to what you just said. I can only imagine what that must be like."

"It's not something I really talk about. I don't know that I've really ever talked about it before." She scowled, squared up to his face, looking him eye to eye, and said, "Do you do this with every girl you meet?"

"No. I'm friends with plenty of women that have never went beyond friendship."

"That's not what I mean. I'm talking about the women you date and are intimate with."

"Yes and no. Does the interaction always elicit the emotional processing that's happening right now? No. But do I try to facilitate a clear space between us. Yes. I can't really bring myself to being engaged in a depth of intimacy otherwise. I desire deep connection more than I desire sex." He laughed, "I mean, don't get me wrong. Sex is great. I love me some sex. But," he said with emphasis, "I desire deep connection more. And emotional vulnerability is what I've found to facilitate that deep connection best."

"You really are a hippy, aren't you?"

He just smiled.

More From Michael Phoenix

- On Eros
  - Sēnsuālitās, vol. 2
  - Sublīmātiō, vol. 3
- Of the First Magnitude
  - Facing Revelation: An Emerging, vol. 1
  - iRise: An Algorhythm of Freedom, vol. 2
  - Quantum Engineering: Introspecting the Rabbit Hole, vol. 3
  - Algorhythmic Insight: Poetic Analysis of the Journey, vol. 4
- Body Integration & the One Minute Workout: Learning to Love the Body You're In